Frank and Bert

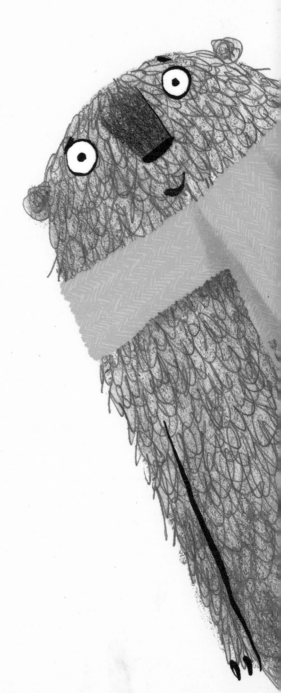

For Steve Adams –
a fabulous friend x

First published in 2022 by Nosy Crow Ltd
Wheat Wharf, 27a Shad Thames, London, SE1 2XZ, UK

Nosy Crow Eireann Ltd
44 Orchard Grove, Kenmare, Co Kerry, V93 FY22, Ireland

www.nosycrow.com

ISBN 978 1 78800 840 2 (HB)
ISBN 978 1 78800 841 9 (PB)

A CIP catalogue record for this book is available from the British Library.

Printed in China
Papers used by Nosy Crow are made from wood grown in sustainable forests.

3 5 7 9 10 8 6 4 2 (HB)
5 7 9 10 8 6 (PB)

Frank and Bert

Chris Naylor-Ballesteros

Hello, I'm Frank.

This is me and my best friend, Bert.

We love to play hide-and-seek.
Bert thinks he's brilliant at hiding –
but he isn't.

He's **terrible** at it!

Here's what happens.
I close my eyes and
count to ten.

1 2 3 4 5 6 7 8 9

10!

"Here I come,
ready or not!"

And there he is!

Or he's there, as plain as day!

Do you see what I mean?

But Bert says I always find him because
he doesn't get enough time to hide properly.

He would **really** love to win at hide-and-seek,
even if it was just once.

Well, I **really** love winning **too**, but
I decide to give my best friend a chance
and count to a **hundred**.

Which takes a **long** time.

I start counting . . .

and off Bert runs . . .

1 2 3 4 5 6 7 8 9 10 11 12 13

97 98 99 100!

"Here I come, Bert,
ready or not!"

Straight away,

I find a clue.

And I'm sure that when I get to the end . . .

I'll find a rock or a tree or something like that, hiding . . .

...a
bear
behind
it!

I've won again!

I'm about to reach out
and pull Bert's tail . . .

. . . but I stop.

Bert is going to be very sad if he loses again.

And even though I **love** winning,
I **love** my best friend **more!**

So . . .

I take a deep breath and shout . . .

"BERT . . .

. . . I GIVE UP!

Where are you?"

And out he pops!

The happiest bear in the world.

My best friend, Bert, has won at last.

Now we're back home and I'm fixing Bert's scarf,
so he's ready to play another day.

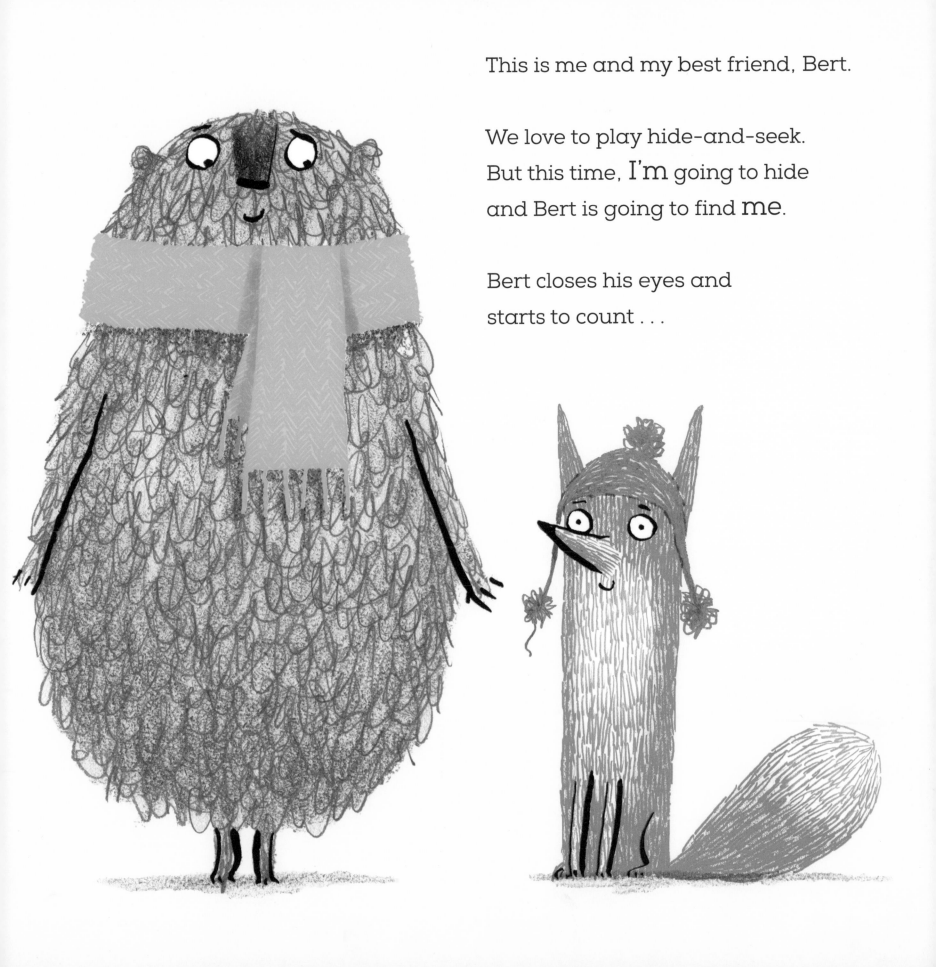

This is me and my best friend, Bert.

We love to play hide-and-seek.
But this time, I'm going to hide
and Bert is going to find me.

Bert closes his eyes and
starts to count . . .

. . . and off I run.

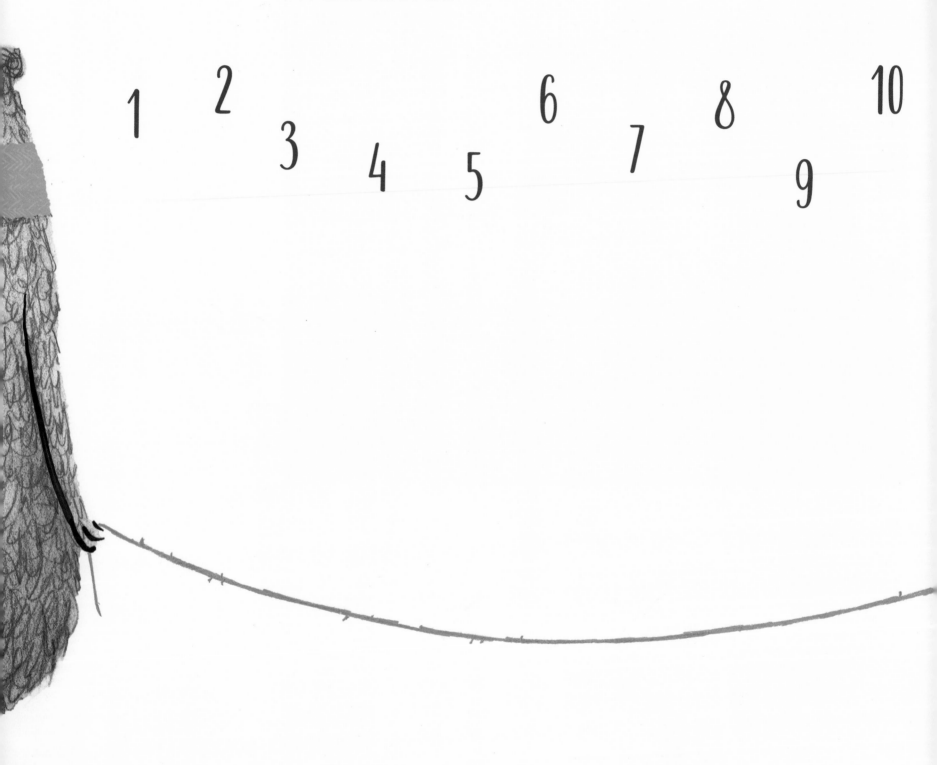

11 12 13 14 15 16 17 18 19 20…

He'll **NEVER** find me!